What People
A Christmas Story You've Never Heard

"It's the Christmas story minus the hazy glow of history and distance. See Mary and Joseph as their contemporaries saw them: a knocked-up local girl and the disgrace-of-a-man desperate enough to marry her. Find out who can handle a work of God and who is too damned religious to deal with its impropriety." — **Jennifer Ramsey**

"How many times have I heard the Christmas story? Then I listened to Real Live Preacher's version, and that old, old story became new and fresh again!" — **Cindy Aasen**

"This is the greatest story ever told, and RLP brings it to life by adding the one thing that's always been missing: human emotion."
—**Terry Simmons**

"A true literary masterpiece. I think everyone in the whole world should own a copy." —**RLP's mother**

"Real Live Preacher takes a dusty story we've all heard a hundred times and makes it fresh again." **Sean McMains**
http://www.mcmains.net/ruminations

"It's the Christmas Story for the rest of us. It put me in the middle of the story like no other." —**Xyp**

"Why should you care what a liberal, yahoo, cry-baby, Baptist preacher from Texas has to say about Jesus in the manger? You probably shouldn't. Unless, of course, you couldn't think of anything better to buy your girlfriend for Christmas." —**Jason Kranzusch**
http://axegrinder.blogspot.com

"RLP brings the sketchy outlines of a story found in the Gospels to life in a way that few would have the courage to attempt. My heart pounded with Joseph's as he searched for somewhere for his betrothed to give birth to their child. You'll want to share this with everyone you know."
—**Casey Rousseau**

"Don't judge a book by it's cover . . . unless that cover has an advertisement for the author's own webpage on it." —**K.C. Flynn**

"After 7 years of Catholic Schools, 5 years of Catechism, 30 years of attending church, and 8 years working at a Methodist church, I finally experienced the Christmas story. Beautiful. warm. loving." —**Kari Knudson**

"'Joseph's carpenter shed smelled of leather and wood and earth and grease and work.' Right from the opening sentence this story puts your senses into the question of the ages. 'Who are you my little Jesus Boy? Who ARE you?'" —**Idle Pilgrim**

"The ideal gift for someone who is looking for the real story!"
—**Dan Bowman**
http://thetimesink.net/Blog/

"A Christmas Story You've Never Heard is sweet, sincere and somewhat surprising, like a tail-wagging puppy who just wee'd in your bed."
—**Christy Howard**

"Real Live Preacher puts the drama, the scandal, and the humanity back into the Christmas story. Familiarity and remoteness evaporated as I read it, and before my eyes the Word became flesh." —**Jacob**
twentyfeet.blogspot.com

"In all the crèches and pageants I've seen there are always kings, shepherds and animals. What's missing are the dung and the flies. That's why I appreciate RLP's writing. He's not afraid to touch the more earthy parts of life we often keep neatly tucked out of sight." —**Ramblin' Dan**
http://www.thehighcalling.org

"So, this is it. The Christmas Story You've Never Heard. Thank God you'll never have to hear it now! You can read it silently to yourself."
—**Melanie Stivers**

"You'll find yourself laughing, crying, cursing, and inviting friends to read this amazing story . . . then realizing that it is, in fact, the one you hear every year – just never like this!" —**Shaun O'reilly**
www.thoseawake.com

"It's the Christmas Story as you've never heard it, written in the inimitable style of Real Live Preacher. RLP wasn't actually present at the birth of Jesus, but when you read this story, you will find that hard to believe."
—**Quaker Lady**

"Most TV Preachers and famous Pastors will hate this story. That's why you should read it." —**Jimmy Chalmers**

A CHRISTMAS STORY YOU'VE NEVER HEARD

Gordon Atkinson

San Antonio, Texas
2006

Copyright 2006 © by Gordon Atkinson
All rights reserved

Published for Consafo.com
by Watercress Press
San Antonio

Cover art by Robert Lovato.
Illustrations by Steve Erspanner.
Book design by Fishead Design Studio.

ISBN 10: 0-9788880-0-6
ISBN 13: 978-0-9788880-0-8

DEDICATION

Special thanks to Ben, Drew, Elizabeth,
John, and Frannie.

For the people of Covenant, who first heard
this story many years ago.
For Jeanene, who loves me.
And for the three sisters.

CONTENTS

Preface	viii
About the Author	ix
Introduction	1
Part One: The Census	7
Part Two: The Plan	17
Part Three: The Journey	27
Part Four: The Rejection	37
Part Five: The Angels	47
Part Six: The Manger	57
Part Seven: The Shepherds	67
Part Eight: The Question	77

PREFACE

This is a work of fiction based on events described in the second chapter of Luke. It is the first in a planned series of seven dramatized versions of the gospel stories surrounding the birth of Jesus.

One cannot imagine the birth of Jesus without making a lot of assumptions. The assumptions of my Christmas story are very different from those that have become traditional, but there is nothing wrong with that. Sometimes it is good to look at a story in a new way.

The specific details of this story are my own invention, but let us never forget that their lives were as full of details and dialogue as our own.

ABOUT THE AUTHOR

Gordon Atkinson is the pastor of Covenant Baptist Church in San Antonio, Texas. He writes regularly for The Christian Century and The High Calling, a non-profit organization in San Antonio. His weblog, Real Live Preacher, has been in existence since 2002.

Gordon and his wife have three daughters and as many vocations. They try to take things one day at a time.

A CHRISTMAS STORY
YOU'VE NEVER HEARD

INTRODUCTION

Luke 2:1-7

And it came to pass in those days, that there went out a decree from Caesar Augustus, that all the world should be taxed. This taxing was first made when Cyrenius was governor of Syria.) And all went to be taxed, every one into his own city. And Joseph also went up from Galilee, out of the city of Nazareth, into Judaea, unto the city of David, which is called Bethlehem; (because he was of the house and lineage of David:) to be taxed with Mary his espoused wife, being great with child. And so it was, that, while they were there, the days were accomplished that she should be delivered. And she brought forth her firstborn son, and wrapped him in swaddling clothes, and laid him in a manger; because there was no room for them in the inn. (KJV)

The facts are few and the account minimal to the point of absurdity. In a few short verses, Luke tells us everything we know about the birth of Jesus of Nazareth, he who would come to be known as the Christ.

His father traveled sixty miles south from Nazareth to Bethlehem because of a census of some kind. For reasons unknown to us, Joseph brought along his fiancé who was expecting a child at any time. The four to five day walk must have been tough for her.

When they arrived in Bethlehem she went into labor. Whatever accommodations they had hoped for did not work out, so they had to find a place at the last minute. The swaddling clothes were normal, of course, and the trough bed was probably not unheard of either. Mary and Joseph were common people and used to making do with what was at hand.

Introduction

There is wonder and mystery in this story, much of it hiding between the verses and in the silences that cry out to pilgrim readers. Luke's soft words give us the gentle and polite details, but the real story was one of pain and surprise, of grace, beauty, and brutality.

I'm fascinated by how we have filled in the gaps over the years. In building our own Christmas story, we have padded this bare account with cultural details, many of which are anachronistic or simply unlikely.

It is unlikely that Mary rode a donkey in the last stages of her pregnancy. It is unlikely that the census required her to make the journey at all. In her state she could have stayed at home with her mother. Why Joseph brought her is something of a mystery.

There certainly was no inn or innkeeper. The Greek word Luke used was "kataluma," as in, "There was no room for them in the kataluma." Scholars agree that this word describes a spare room of some kind or perhaps a common room for travelers who needed a roof over their heads. On busy nights there would have been several families snoozing in the corners of the village kataluma, covered with blankets and robes.

Most surprising is the truth about the manger. Wooden barns of the type seen in most nativity sets were not known in Judea, where wood was scarce. There are limestone caves nearby that might have housed animals. Certainly mangers would have been there. The truth is, many homes had mangers. Archaeologists have excavated dwellings in the area and discovered that peasant homes often had two levels, the upper for the family and the lower for the animals. A permanent stone trough in the lower part of the house was the most common type of manger.

Finally, three kings did not appear at his birth bringing gifts. The Bible says that magi came, stargazing priests of ancient Persian tradition. The number of magi is not specified, and in any case, they did not arrive until perhaps two years later. By that time, Mary and Joseph had moved into a house. The magi story is from Matthew's gospel and has no real connection to the actual birth of Jesus.

It seems the real Christmas story is lacking many of our favorite elements. Perhaps you are wondering what kind of story might be left without the donkey and the animals in the barn, without the busy but kindly innkeeper, without the rickety manger, and without the stunning gifts lying in the straw.

What kind of story, indeed.

Part One

THE CENSUS

Joseph's carpenter shed smelled of leather and wood and grease and earth and work. The tools were old and the wooden handles slick with use. The place bore the wonderful patina of a man's lifework.

The smell made Isaac smile when he poked his head around the doorframe and saw Joseph's powerful shoulders rolling back and forth as he pulled a drawknife across a huge beam of wood. Chips were flying everywhere.

"Shalom, Joseph. Is that . . . He sniffed loudly. "Cedar?"

Joseph turned and smiled, slapping his palm on the side of the beam. "Yes. Contract with the governor. Man dropped it off just the other day. Very nice wood. From Lebanon!"

"You don't say? Yes, very nice." Isaac ran his hand over the wood with some appreciation for it.

Joseph went back to working, and Isaac looked around the shed in sadness. They used to gather here, all the men. Simeon and Jacob, Josiah and his cousin from Jericho, Jonathan Ben-Judah and the others. Even the rabbi would come by sometimes. This used to be the place where they came to get away from the women and children. This was where they talked together, like men. But that was before the whole "Mary thing."

The Census

Joseph strained with the drawknife, ripping it through a knot as he spoke. "So, Isaac, what's the news? I'm going to keep working, if you don't mind. I've got a deadline."

"Maybe," said Isaac, "but you'll probably stop when you hear what I've got to say." He paused, but Joseph said nothing.

"A government census has been ordered."

"And what's the news in that? Another census, another way for the tax collectors to pick our pockets."

"No, Joseph. Listen. This is an imperial census. Apparently the order comes all the way from Rome. Maybe even from the emperor." Isaac turned his head and spat. "But the worst news is that every man is required to go to his home town to register. His home town, Joseph, and no exceptions.

It's all going to happen midsummer."

Joseph's back straightened, and he whirled around to face Isaac. "Midsummer? But that's when . . ."

"Yes, my friend. That's when Mary is due."

"You know?"

"Of course I know. I have fingers and can count the months. Everyone knows. The whole town is talking."

Joseph picked up a chisel. With a flick of his wrist he sank the sharp corner into the wood and then popped it out. "Yes, I suppose everyone is talking. And I guess that's why none of my friends drop by anymore, right?"

Isaac looked uncomfortable. Joseph stared at him for a moment, then looked down at the wood, picking at it with his thumbnail. "It looks like you have something on your mind, old friend. Go ahead and speak if you have something to say."

"All right, I will. Joseph, you know that I love you like a brother. We've been friends since you came to Nazareth, however long ago. But why are you getting mixed up with that girl? We both know the child isn't yours. She has betrayed you, and no one even knows who the father is. You're an honest man and well respected. You could have any girl in town. Why do you care so much about . . . her and her worthless child?"

"Stop!" shouted Joseph. "Isaac, for the sake of our friendship, I will forget what you just said. But remember this – I will marry her, and the child she bears is mine. That's all you need to know. My son will not grow up thinking that . . ."

"Son?" said Isaac. "What makes you think it will be a boy?"

Joseph walked to the door and looked around to be sure that no one was outside listening. Then he ducked back inside and squatted on the floor, motioning Isaac to join him. Isaac, looking like he was in on a grand conspiracy, lowered himself beside Joseph.

"Isaac, there are things you don't know about Mary. Things no one knows. I don't ask that you understand or even agree with me. Just know that I intend to make the boy my own. I had a dream, or maybe a vision, I don't know. But in this dream . . ." Joseph paused, uncertain of how much to tell his friend. He didn't want people to think he was crazy. He hovered on the edge for a moment, wanting so badly to tell Isaac everything, but then the mood passed, and he decided to keep the details to himself.

"Well, just understand that because of this dream, or whatever it was, I think it will be a boy, and I'm going to raise him as my own."

As he said "raise him as my own," Joseph imagined a little boy playing at his feet. He smiled, but then he had a vision of people whispering, saying that Joseph wasn't really the boy's father. He stood up, trembling, and felt his anger rise, exploding out of his mouth.

"And that's it, Isaac. That's final. That's the way it's going to be, and I don't care what anyone else thinks or says. Do you understand?"

Isaac stood also, and looked angry for a brief moment, then a smile broke over his face. Joseph thought the smile came a little too soon to be genuine.

"Hey, Joseph, it's your life. I'm just your friend. Do what you think is right. But no one trusts that Mary girl. I'm sorry, but that's the truth. Everyone likes you — you know — but do whatever you need to do, I guess."

Isaac walked to the door as if he was going to leave, but he paused in the doorway. He put a hand on each side of the doorframe and leaned forward. Then he turned around and had a final say.

"It's going to be hard on Mary when you're in Bethlehem for the census, that's all I'm saying. People in a small town can be cruel. Are cruel. I heard that her parents were going to send her away, like Hagar, until you agreed to marry her. With you gone, I don't know. It's something to think about, whether or not you want to get mixed up in a situation like that.

"Take care, Joseph," he said, and then he was gone.

Joseph stood for a moment, looking at the empty door. The sun was going down, so he lit a lamp and sat in the corner of his little shed. No one else came to see him.

The Census

He sat for a long time in the shadows, thinking about all these things.

A Christmas Story You've Never Heard

Part Two

THE PLAN

Two days after Joseph spoke with Isaac, he caught Mary's eye outside her parents' house. He gave her "the look," and she nodded to let him know that she understood they were to meet at the usual place and time.

Just as the sun was going down, Joseph made his way to a small grove of ancient olive trees on the edge of town and not far from Mary's home. He loved this place. The trees kept their silence, as always. Their twisted trunks and sagging branches seemed to lend him their dignity and peace. He laid a hand on the rough bark of one of the oldest trees and thought about all that had happened.

This was where he had first seen Mary, about a year earlier. He was passing by when, ever appreciative of good wood, he stopped to look at the trees. Mary chanced upon him, startling them both. They nodded politely and went their separate ways, but Joseph had not been able to get her out of his mind.

Later they met formally at the town well. Meeting your husband or wife at the town well was very biblical and traditional, and it made Joseph feel good to get things started in such a proper fashion. Of course he had orchestrated the whole thing. He found out when Mary was going to be at the well, then he showed up claiming he was there to "water his friend's donkey."

A simple courtship followed, then an engagement agreement was made with her father. After that, they met occasionally in the olive grove to talk and once even to embrace, though such a thing was a little forward and even now made Joseph blush to think of it.

And then everything had taken an unexpected turn. One day Mary looked at him and he understood that he should meet her at the grove that evening. When he arrived she was already there, looking quite frantic. She fell at his feet and begged his forgiveness, telling him about a baby and a mysterious visit from an angel. He stormed off in anger, planning to call off the engagement, only to return a few days later and fall at her feet with his own crazy story to tell.

She saw an angel who told her the child inside her was God's own little boy. He had a dream where an angel told him to believe her and to marry her anyway. They were the only two people who knew of these visions, but everyone else thought they were out of their minds.

Things had been especially hard on Mary. Some people called her a whore, and her parents had even shut her out of the house one evening. That night she stayed in Joseph's shed with his tools and his wood. While she slept he whittled her a tiny angel to help her be strong and believe. She loved the little angel and kept it with her always.

Now, standing in that same olive grove, Joseph shook his head and wondered what he was getting himself into. Then he saw Mary approaching through the trees with a small lamp in her hand. She looked agitated.

"Joseph, have you heard about the census? You're going to have to go to Bethlehem, aren't you? And right when the baby is due. I'm scared to be here without you. I . . . I don't know what my parents will do. What if something terrible happens to me before you come back?"

She looked away for a moment, biting her lip, then pulled her eyes back to meet his.

"You are coming back for me, right? You do still believe in your dream, don't you?

Joseph smiled and held out his arms for her. "Of course I believe in the dream. Am I not named for the greatest dreamer of all, the one whose dreams and visions led our people to Egypt? I've always believed in dreams. This is how God speaks to people in important times."

Mary rushed to him and melted into his chest. They were unashamed of embracing now, though such a thing was frowned upon. Social and religious customs seemed weak and silly in light of what they were facing.

And they were facing a lot. Crazy dreams and visits from angels had convinced them that the baby boy she carried inside her had a very important part to play in God's plan. They understood that they should stand together as his parents, even if that meant standing against their own religious tradition.

And so Joseph stood with Mary in the olive grove and told her his plan.

Mary would come to Bethlehem with him, in spite of the fact that she would be near the end of her pregnancy by the time they could leave. It was crazy, he knew, but he thought they could pull it off. They would take six or seven days for the journey instead of the usual four. They would cut straight through Samaria to save time, walking slowly and making their way from village to village.

When they got to Bethlehem, Joseph's family would take care of them. His parents lived there, as did a couple of brothers and some extended family. They would assume that Joseph had gotten Mary pregnant before their marriage. They would be disappointed, but such things happened from time to time. If they assured his family that they planned to be married as soon as possible, they would be accepted after some scolding and a lecture or two.

Mary was stunned. The idea that she would bear her first child away from her mother and the familiar women of the village was very frightening. "I don't know, Joseph. It's very scary. Are you sure we're going to be okay?"

Joseph was not a man to make foolish promises. He exhaled loudly and told the truth.

"No, Mary, I'm not certain we'll be okay. To tell you the truth, I'm not sure of anything anymore. We're in uncharted territory, and I've lost sight of all the familiar paths. We've left religion itself behind, you might say. It's not like the Torah is going to show us the way, exactly."

He looked thoughtful, and they were both silent for a moment. Then he spoke again.

"Although, I do seem to recall that some of the greatest women of our faith often found themselves in, shall we say, 'interesting' predicaments. I mean, there was Rahab, who . . . well, you know. And Lot's daughters — oh my God! And there was Ruth; don't forget Ruth. She and Boaz . . . well . . . and she was a gentile! And Rahab too, she was a gentile. And what about Queen Esther? She didn't exactly live the life of an innocent Jewish girl, and yet God used her to save our people. None of these women were exactly pure in the eyes of their neighbors, if you know what I mean."

Joseph's eyes began to sparkle with excitement. He looked at Mary in a new way.

"Mary, did your father ever sing to you before the Sabbath? Did he ever sing, 'May you be like Ruth and like Esther?'"

Mary's smile lit up her face. "Yes," she said.

"Okay then, you are like Ruth and like Esther. To me you are, anyway. Maybe we only have God on our side, but that's enough, isn't it?

"As I see it, the only path the Lord seems to have left for us is taking us right to Bethlehem."

A Christmas Story You've Never Heard

Part Three

THE JOURNEY

If Mary had any misgivings about leaving Nazareth and having her baby in Bethlehem among strangers, the months leading up to their departure erased all doubt from her mind. She and Joseph became social outcasts, one-dimensional characters. She was the "bad girl" who got pregnant, and he was the "desperate fool" who was going to marry her anyway.

Some people stared and whispered. Others gave them nasty looks or pulled their children tightly into their robes if Mary or Joseph walked by.

Though they originally wanted to return to Nazareth after the baby was born, they soon decided it would be better just to start a new life in Bethlehem. So Joseph finished what work he had, and then sold his tools across the Jordan in the Decapolis, where they didn't care who was pregnant or how she got that way. He planned to buy new tools in Judea and practice his trade after they were settled in Bethlehem.

And so, early one morning Joseph packed his donkey with everything they owned, shouldered a hefty pack, and led Mary out of Nazareth just as the first rays of sunlight could be seen in the Eastern sky. They tried to be quiet as they weaved between the sleepy houses. The only sound they made was when Mary wept as she passed her childhood home.

No one knew they were leaving, and no one would have said good-bye if they had. It was one of the more ironic moments in history. Two lowly outcasts slipped out of town unnoticed, beginning a journey that would end with the birth of the most important and influential human ever to walk the planet.

And though it was the journey that frightened them in the beginning, it was in Bethlehem that they would learn there are worse things in life than whispering neighbors. Much worse.

The trip itself was not terribly difficult. They were young and strong, having known nothing but walking and hard work all of their lives. They kept a slow pace, traveling about ten miles a day and taking frequent rests.

Leaving Nazareth, they moved south, passing near Nain and through Jezreel, spending the second night in Jeblaam, on the border of Samaria. They were both nervous about passing through Samaria, having been taught to fear and loathe Samaritans since childhood. But they were surprised to find the villagers of that region to be gentle and kind.

In fact, it was in Samaria that they came to understand the power of a pregnant woman. They had only to come limping into a village — which was usually nothing more than a scattering of earthen homes — and the local women would flock to Mary's aid. There would be some clucking and scolding, some outrage that she was traveling in her condition, but they were always given food, drink, and shelter for the night if needed.

Joseph, who had some knowledge of the law, offered silent prayers for forgiveness because of the impurity of the food, but he counted Mary's health as the most important thing. He vowed to offer a hundred sacrifices in Jerusalem one day if only God would keep Mary and the baby safe.

For her part, Mary never forgot the kindness of the Samaritan people. It was in Samaria where she first received acceptance for her child, and she reveled in the nurturing attention. Years later, when she told her son the story of his birth, she always spoke kindly of the Samaritans who welcomed them when they were strangers.

The most memorable event of the journey happened near the Samaritan village of Sychar, close to Mount Gerazim. They stopped at the famous Well of Jacob and were remembering their own meeting at the well in Nazareth, which seemed like years before. Mary told Joseph that she never believed that line about him needing to water someone's donkey. They were still laughing when a beautiful Samaritan woman came to the well. When she smiled at the two of them, the baby kicked so violently that Mary gasped and held her stomach. The woman rushed over and put one hand on Mary's back. She then moved her other hand slowly toward her bulging tummy, looking into Mary's eyes to see if it was okay. When Mary smiled, the woman laid her hand softly on the roundness of her belly. She closed her eyes and proclaimed the child to be very strong indeed. Joseph felt the happiness that is a man's pride, then he felt a rush of emotion as he realized that he was beginning to feel like a father.

On the fifth day they crossed the southern Samaritan border and entered Judea. They spent that night in the ancient city of Shiloh where Hannah had cried out to the Lord for a child. They continued to travel slowly, finally drawing within sight of the

The Journey

holy city of Jerusalem on the morning of the seventh day.

Normally they would have passed through Jerusalem, enjoying the sights and perhaps even visiting the temple, but Joseph was in a hurry now. The ancient lands of Judah were familiar to him, and he was itching to see his home. They took a goatherd path around Jerusalem to the west and drew close to Bethlehem in the late afternoon. Joseph could feel his heart beating when they got near his hometown. He was, after all, a proud son of the House of David, and Bethlehem was in his blood.

Out of respect for David, all the young boys in Joseph's family tended sheep. It was an informal rite of passage, you might say. As a young shepherd, Joseph had roamed the hills and shallow valleys all around Bethlehem, and he still remembered every path and cove. Now he had a surprise for Mary. He led her toward Bethlehem on an old sheep trail, coming in from the northwest in such a way that her view of the city was blocked by a good-sized hill.

They took a rest, at his suggestion, behind a clump of cedar on the side of the hill. Mary looked deeply tired and asked, "How much farther is it?"

Joseph smiled and helped her to her feet. "Not far now," he said, taking her by the hand. He led her around the cedar, and she gasped to find Bethlehem laid out before her eyes on a hillside across a little valley. Earth-colored buildings were clumped together, spilling over the side of a large hill, with smaller dwellings dotting the ground around the city in no apparent order. Here and there little boys could be seen running after sheep, gathering their flocks for the coming night.

Mary was speechless with joy. Joseph nodded, "Pretty, isn't it? Welcome to Bethlehem, the City of David and my . . . our home."

The trip across the little valley seemed like the longest part of their journey, but they finally found themselves winding their way through the haphazard streets of the ancient town. Roads, paths, and alleys sprouted in every direction, but Joseph knew the way and led them to a quiet corner of the city. And finally they stood before the door of his parents' home.

Joseph exhaled powerfully, letting his shoulders sag. He had not been able to relax since they left Nazareth. He touched Mary's cheek and said, "We're home."

A Christmas Story You've Never Heard

Part Four

THE REJECTION

Two hours after they arrived in Bethlehem, Mary and Joseph were wandering the streets in a state of shock and panic. Joseph's family had heard all about their "situation" when a traveler from Nazareth passed through a month or so before.

Joseph could imagine the conversation.

"So, I understand you're from Nazareth, huh?"

"Yeah. Just in town for a few days."

"You wouldn't happen to know a cousin of mine, name of Joseph? Carpenter?"

"Sure, know him well. Used to do some business with him. He built my brother's boat. Fine carpenter. It's a shame, all that's happened — he's obviously lost his mind. You hate to see that kind of thing."

"What are you talking about?"

"You mean you haven't heard about the girl?"

And that was that. His family knew everything.

They were horrified. No illegitimate child had ever been born into their family, and they were shocked that Joseph dared to bring the woman into their own city and right to his parents' front door.

"Like they were just regular people, you know? Right to the front door they came, and knocked. 'Hello, it's our long-lost son

The Rejection

and his slut.' And her hiding around the corner like she was ashamed. Where was her shame when she was sleeping with everyone, I'd like to know. The father's probably a gentile. You know Galilee."

"You expect that kind of thing goes on up in Nazareth, but to bring her here? Right into Judea? Right into the City of David? It's an outrage!"

The family would not allow him into any of their homes. Joseph stood in the alley and argued with his cousin Solomon for almost an hour. Solomon was the only one who would even speak with him, and all he did was deliver the message in no uncertain terms. "You are not welcome here."

When the door finally slammed and Joseph was left standing in the alley, the enormity of their situation began to sink in. They had no money. All that he had gotten for his tools was in a locked box coming south on a hired caravan. It wouldn't arrive for another week or two. He had no friends in town, and now he had no family. They had nowhere to stay, and the baby could come at any time.

"The baby!" thought Joseph. "Mary!" he shouted. Completely humiliated, she had gone around the corner to avoid the vicious looks from Joseph's family. She was sitting against a wall, staring into space. She had heard everything.

They spent the first two nights in the local "Let-Down," or "Kataluma," as the Greeks called it. It was nothing more than a simple room with a dirt floor where travelers relaxed, rather like a bus stop in the modern world. It was crowded because a good number of people were in town for the census.

Joseph and Mary slept sitting against a wall with their robes pulled over them for

The Rejection

privacy. There were at least twenty people in the room, with others sleeping outside. Mary hardly slept that first night because she was so afraid and because a man in the room had a terrible cough. She was also starting to have some intermittent pain, a kind of tightening across her stomach. This was her first pregnancy, so she didn't know what this was, exactly. She said nothing, hoping the pain would go away on its own.

During the day, Joseph scoured the city, looking for temporary work and some kind of accommodations. He found a few rooms they could rent, but no one would believe his story about the money coming on the caravan. And there was no work to be had anywhere.

This was the first time in his life that Joseph was utterly powerless. He had no money, no safety net, no backup plan, and no friends to call on. His helplessness burned in his gut, producing a deep, throbbing anger. He knew that he had to find shelter, and he knew that Mary was going to need help from a woman very soon.

On the second day, when their food ran out, his anger turned to panic. Joseph began to run through the streets. Buildings and houses all looked the same to him; he couldn't remember where he had been. He had a wild look in his eyes, and people shied away from him. One man said, "You've already been here twice, you crazy fool. I have no work for you, and I don't give to filthy beggars. Go on, get out of here!"

Normally Bethlehem would have been a friendlier place, but with all the travelers and the census officials in town, the people were more callous and suspicious than usual.

Joseph's panic was like a drug, causing his heart to beat faster and his mind to race. His breath came in quick gasps, and he

The Rejection

began to have crazy thoughts. He wondered about stealing money or finding money. He kept his eyes on the ground, hoping to find a lost coin. He went back to his parents house a couple of times and stood trembling outside the door, but he couldn't bring himself to knock again.

As the day drew to a close, the unthinkable happened. Mary went into labor. For a couple of hours she was able to stay silent. She tried to tell herself the pain was something else, anything but the baby. Then her denial was swept away by waves of sharp pain that ripped through her midsection. This little boy was coming, whether the world was ready or not. Mary's whimpers became screams. She writhed on the floor, babbling nonsense and pleading for help.

The people in the Kataluma that day were mostly men. There were a couple of younger women, but they had no idea what to do. As Joseph was heading back to check on Mary, he heard her screams from out in the alley and rushed inside. All the travelers had backed up against the walls and were watching Mary, who was clutching her belly in agony.

He was utterly exhausted, but Joseph found the strength to scoop Mary up in his arms and carry her into the street. The sun was almost down and Joseph had only one card to play. The Wildman. He carried Mary down the street, kicking on doors and screaming at the top of his lungs. "Someone help us! Please, we're having a baby!"

No one seemed to hear them. Darkness had fallen, and people were shut safely in their homes. Joseph staggered down the street, but he had been running on panic and adrenaline for most of the day, and exhaustion was setting in. Finally he sank to his knees and laid Mary on the ground.

The Rejection

This was their moment of greatest need. Joseph sat on his knees with Mary's head in his lap. With a voice that was failing, he cried out to God.

"Help us, Adonai, Father in Heaven. You sent angels once . . . please. Help us now. We are Joseph and Mary, and we have no one to turn to but you. We have nothing, but only you."

A Christmas Story You've Never Heard

Part Five

THE ANGELS

Angels appear, now and again, in the pages of the Bible. Angels are messengers, bringers of tidings and good news. They are not the fluffy, winged characters that are popular images in our culture. Apparently, angels were quite frightening.

And then sometimes they look like regular people, and no one recognizes them at all.

The writer of Hebrews thought this a serious enough matter that he gave this dire warning: "You better be kind to strangers, because some have entertained angels and never known it."

On the night Joseph and Mary lay despairing in a Bethlehem street—in fact, at the moment of their deepest need—an angel happened to be walking through that very town. His name was Elias, and he had no idea he was an angel. He would have been shocked had anyone suggested such a thing.

But he was an angel. He was very much an angel on this night.

Every shepherd in and around Bethlehem knew Elias and his wife Esther. Elias had been a shepherd himself in his younger days, back when his bones could handle the walking and the hard work. He was retired, you might say. He and Esther lived in a modest little home on the edge of town.

The Angels

Elias lived a quiet life now, doing odd jobs and tending to the birthing of lambs. He and Esther still kept busy, but in different ways. There were grandchildren constantly underfoot, friends who dropped by to chat, and animals to care for. Sometimes Elias would visit the shepherds in the field. He liked to sit by the fire and tell them stories of the old days.

On this particular night he had visited a young shepherd's home to check on an ailing lamb. They fed him for his trouble, and with his belly full he was in a good mood, whistling as he walked home. He rounded a corner and almost stumbled over Joseph cradling Mary in his lap in the middle of a narrow lane.

"Hey, watch out there young fella. Why are you out here in the middle of the street?"

Joseph was startled to hear a voice and

jumped to his feet. He grabbed Elias by his robes. "Please, help us. My wife is having a baby . . . right now. And we're from far away, out of town. And I guess we don't know anyone, so do you know anyone?"

Elias knelt to get a closer look at Mary. "Hold on there, now. You're from out of town, you say? Ain't you got nobody to help you?"

"No, no. That's what I'm saying. We don't have anyone. We thought we did, but . . . I have money, only it's not here. It'll be here in a couple of weeks, I promise, but suddenly the baby was coming, and I couldn't find anyone or anyplace. Look, none of that matters now, only just, do you know someone who can help us? The baby is coming, see?"

Elias laid a hand on Mary's tummy and looked down, almost like he was listening. She was between contractions, breathing hard, but alert. He watched her seriously for a moment, then smiled and looked up at Joseph.

"This here's your first, ain't it?"

Joseph nodded.

Elias laughed. "Heehee, I can always tell." He looked back at Mary, serious again. "Okay, girlie, you tell old Elias. How long has the pain been real bad?"

Mary thought for a moment. "A couple of hours, I guess."

"Okay, listen now. This is important. Has any water poured out of you?"

Mary was embarrassed and shook her head.

Joseph looked alarmed and bent down to look closely at Mary. "We'd of seen that, right?"

"Hell yes, you'd of seen it. I think you would see a bucket of water come pouring down her legs, wouldn't you?"

He looked once more at Mary and then stood up, rubbing his hands together. "Nah, you kids got time. Now listen here, sweetheart. You sit still a moment, till you get to feeling like you could stand. When the pain comes again, you squeeze your man's hand hard, and go ahead and scream. It don't make no matter how loud neither, understand? And when you're ready, we'll get you up and walking. I'm taking you home. My Esther will take care of you. I guess she's birthed, I don't know, hundreds of babies."

He looked away and upwards, with his lips moving like he was figuring numbers. "Yeah, got to be hundreds, by now."

A sudden rush of violent relief unloosed something in Joseph. He lost control of himself for a moment, and his body shook with racking sobs. Elias looked away politely.

When he was finished, Joseph took a couple of deep breaths and said, "Thank you, Elias. I don't even know how to . . . You came at just the right moment. We didn't . . . I don't know what we were going to do. I don't know anything about babies or . . ."

Elias cut Joseph off with a wave of his hand. "Well, now you forget all that. We didn't have much choice, did we? We couldn't let little missy have her baby in the middle of this alley, now could we?" He snorted. "Course not!"

He said, "we." He said it, and Joseph thought he had never heard a word more beautiful. They were alone, but Elias came, and now they were "we."

Joseph got his donkey and pack, and they began walking to Elias' home. It was a terrible journey. Every so often the contractions would come, and Mary would have to sit down in the street and find a way to get through the pain. Elias rolled up a piece of cloth for her to bite on and told her to breathe a lot. While they were walking, he told her about Esther to keep her mind off her misery.

"Don't you worry, little one. Like I said, Esther's birthed hundreds of children. She loves them. and she's got a soft spot for young mothers, too. Especially first-timers. She'll take good care of you. Like she was your own mother."

Tears welled up in Mary's eyes when Elias said, "your own mother." She looked at Joseph, who nodded sadly, bit his lip, and looked away.

The walk only took an hour, but it seemed like forever. Finally Elias told them they were getting close. At one point he stopped and whistled loudly. A woman's face appeared in the window of a small house.

"Sarah, we got a woman having a baby here. They're strangers, and they got

The Angels

nowhere to go. Hustle down to my house, would you, sweetheart, and tell Esther we got an emergency coming."

The girl ran off in the darkness. Elias looked at Joseph and said, "Sweet girl, that Sarah. Little simple, maybe, but a helluva good cook. Don't you worry; Esther will be ready for us."

At last they came within sight of Elias' home. It was a simple, one-room house with a flat roof. A woman was silhouetted in the doorway, holding a lamp. Elias left Mary with Joseph and ran to the door. He spoke briefly with the woman, then turned back and shouted, "This is Esther." The woman nodded at them and took charge.

"Sarah, help me get this young woman . . . what's your name, sweetheart?"

"It's Mary," Joseph said.

"Yes, thank you, dear. Sarah, help me get

Mary into the house, and then run find Hannah and Judith. Tell them what's happened. They'll know what to bring."

Esther and Sarah helped Mary into the house. Joseph started to follow, but Elias caught him by the sleeve. "Hey there, young fella. You and I'll stay out here. Come over to my shed; we'll sit and have some wine. You listen here, now. Mary will be fine. She's in Esther's hands, and Esther . . . . well . . . Esther knows all what to do."

Elias looked at the door to his house, now closed, and nodded with pride and confidence.

"I promise you this, there's no better place in all the world for your Mary to be than right here."

Part Six

THE MANGER

Elias got a lamp and led Joseph to a small shed near his house. The lamplight revealed dusty piles of fleece and wool in the corners, worn shepherd gear hanging on the walls, and the inevitable curved staff leaning in the corner.

Using the lamp, Elias started a fire in a small earthen stove. Then he pulled a wineskin off the wall and handed it to Joseph. There was a flash of movement visible through the door, and they saw two women running toward the house.

Elias brought his chin up quickly and then back down. "That would be Hannah and Judith," he said. The door to the house opened, spilling light into the darkness. The women slipped inside, and the door shut behind them.

Joseph swallowed a mouthful of wine and sat down on a bench near the door of the shed where he could keep an eye on the house. He ran a hand through his hair, exhaled deeply, and leaned his head back against the doorframe. He closed his eyes, intending to rest for a moment, but he was soon snoring softly.

He awoke with a start when he heard whispering. He saw Sarah slipping out the door into the darkness. Elias noticed he was awake and grinned. "Sarah's brought something to eat," He said. He rolled up two pieces of flatbread, tied a string around each, and laid them in the opening of the oven.

"I'll just warm them up. I'm sure you're hungry after all you been through."

"Yeah," said Joseph, yawning. "Thanks. How long does this usually take, anyway?"

"Birthing? There's no telling. This being her first, it might be awhile. Then again, she's been walking a lot. You been asleep longer than you think, too. Could be a few hours. Could be longer. Could be anytime now."

Joseph rolled his head around, stretching his neck. He took a quick look at the house, then bumped the back of his head on the doorframe a few times. He looked over at Elias who was poking at the bread rolls with a stick.

"You know, I grew up here," said Joseph. "I left when I was seventeen. Went to Nazareth with my uncle to learn carpentry.

Long story. Anyway, I used to do some shepherding when I was a boy, but I don't remember you."

Elias nodded. "Yeah, we came here about fifteen years ago. Something like that. I used to do a lot of work around Jerusalem. My master brought us to Bethlehem to look after his sheep. Our whole family came. It's nice here; we like it fine."

Joseph nodded. Elias pulled the bread rolls from the oven and handed one to Joseph who grunted his thanks. It was filled with meat, and he ate it with gusto, wiping his hands on his robe when he was done. He wished he had another one.

Elias pushed the last bite into this mouth and walked over to the doorway. He stood beside Joseph, chewing, while the two of them watched the door of the house. He swallowed, hit his chest a couple of times with his fist, then belched.

"You're in town for the census, right?"

"Yeah."

"I thought so. I seen a number of people in town for that. Mighty inconvenient if you ask me. I don't understand any of it." He paused a moment, then spoke again.

"What about your family? They ain't here in town no more? How is it this is your hometown and you got no place to stay? And, if you don't mind me saying, it's a funny thing, taking your wife on a journey when she's just about to deliver. You know, I'm sure you got your reasons, but . . ."

Joseph was silent for a moment, looking for words and trying to think just how much he wanted to tell this stranger. "She's not my wife . . . yet. There's problems with family all around. We didn't expect to be without a place to stay, but . . . well, we just got surprised is all. I made some assumptions I shouldn't have."

"Oh, you got family problems. I've seen it before. Had a few myself. Well, none of that makes me no never-mind. What's done is done, and we just gotta make sure this little one gets here safely."

Joseph grunted in a way that sounded like agreement, and the two of them fell silent again.

Elias' face suddenly brightened. "Hey, I didn't tell you about the manger, did I?"

"Manger?"

"Yeah, manger. Okay, when we first came here, I was doing a lot of shepherding. Keeping long hours. I was stronger then, and . . . well, anyway our kids was mostly grown, so Esther was a little lonely. We didn't know that many people yet. So I got her this little lamb, see? She loved it like a pet, you know, like in that one story that Nathan told David?"

Joseph nodded.

The Manger

"Yeah, she did love that little lamb." Elias paused for a moment, lost in a world that was gone. "Huh! That little critter." He took a deep breath.

"Well, anyway I gathered up some stones and built a trough for that lamb. Sturdy one, too, right there in the house. And that was nice, it was, but eventually the lamb turned into a sheep, as lambs will do. Then the grandchildren started coming. So Esther lined that manger with soft cloth and whatnot, and it made a perfect little bed for those grandbabies."

Elias laced his fingers together and put his hands behind his head, leaning back into them, smiling. "I got eleven grandchildren now, and every one of them slept in that little manger. And I got to tell you, sorry as I am for your troubles of course, I think it's gonna be nice to see a little one sleeping there again. I don't guess Esther and me will live long enough to see great-grandchildren, so . . ."

Something tickled the edge of Joseph's mind, and he sat up straight. Things seemed very quiet. "What time of night is it, you think?"

Elias rolled his head around until he could see the moon. His lips moved a bit, then he said, "Oooh, long about the middle of the night, I'd say."

Without any prompting, both of them turned to look at the door to the house. Suddenly it opened, and Esther stood in the light, beckoning them to come over. Joseph jumped to his feet and ran to her. Elias stretched and came at a more dignified pace.

Esther grasped Joseph's hands in her own and said, "Joseph, you're the father of a fine, healthy baby boy!"

"Hey, what did I tell you?" shouted Elias,

trotting the last few steps over and clapping him on the back. Joseph felt a rush of relief and excitement, but he was subdued around strangers. He nodded his head up and down in an exaggerated motion. He said nothing, but a single staccato laugh burst out of his lips.

He started to move past Esther into the house, but she stopped him. "Now Joseph, Mary's asleep and needs to sleep. The baby's lying over there in that manger. I know that seems odd, but. . ."

Elias broke in. "I told him all about the manger, Esther. Come on now and let this man inside to see his son."

Esther stepped back and Joseph hurried past her. She and Elias paused in the door, and she whispered in his ear. "It's good to see a little one in that manger again, isn't it?"

"Yes, ma'am," he said, pulling her close.

A Christmas Story You've Never Heard

Part Seven

THE SHEPHERDS

The shepherds hit the town at about two o'clock in the morning, and you can be sure there was hell to pay at the next council meeting where there was some dispute about exactly what happened. According to some, they had banged on doors and dragged decent folk out of their beds. They were running up and down the streets singing strange songs and babbling about angels, babies, and peace on earth.

Admittedly, these were the more extreme accounts.

Others said the shepherds had been drinking heavily that night, and things had just gotten a little out of hand. As one man put it, "Shepherds will be shepherds."

The truth is probably somewhere in the middle. What is known for sure is that a dozen or so shepherds came rushing into town sometime in the middle of the night. They were mostly young men, which was understandable since the younger shepherds usually had the night shift.

It seems clear that some of the shepherds did bang on doors and try to awaken people, though it's doubtful that anyone was actually dragged from bed. They had a difficult time explaining themselves to the few sleepy citizens who were willing to come outside. Shepherds are not exactly known for their verbal skills.

Apparently some of them thought there was an army of angels singing on the hillside.

The Shepherds

One or two said there was one angel with a message, but agreed that a whole gang of angels joined in later. There was some mention of a baby, but no one ever made sense of that part. They denied accusations that they were simply drinking and brawling, though the mud on their robes and the straw in their hair certainly made it look as though they'd been rolling on the ground.

There was one older man among them, a shepherd named Mordecai, who was supposed to have been watching the boys that night. He might have shed some light on these events, but he was unable to speak, having lost his voice back on the hillside where something terribly frightening had obviously occurred.

They made quite a commotion in town, that much was certain. And they never backed down from their crazy story either, though no one ever figured out exactly what that story was. In the end, everyone cursed them soundly and went back to bed. And, as mentioned before, the subject was addressed in some detail and with no small amount of passion at the next town council meeting.

On the night in question, after the failed attempt to arouse and alert their neighbors, the shepherds gathered at Mordecai's home to decide what was to be done. Mordecai was unable to join in the discussion, but he pounded on the table and gave exaggerated nods whenever a good point was made.

In the end they managed to agree on a few things. First, there had indeed been a stranger among them. Initially they had not realized he was an angel, but his voice cleared up all doubts on that point. It was around this time that Mordecai lost the ability to speak.

Second, the angel told them about a savior, or a messiah, or a king, or at least someone very important. There was heated debate on the details of this message, but they did agree that this important person had been born in Bethlehem that very night. For reasons not made clear by the angel, this child was lying in a sheep trough somewhere in town. There was complete agreement on this last point.

Third, a choir of angels sang heavenly songs to close out the evening. The sheer beauty of this singing had reduced them all to blubbering idiots.

Apparently the bawling had wiped out whatever was left of Mordecai's already strained voice.

Finally, they agreed that they needed to find this child and see him for themselves, if only to make sure they hadn't lost their minds. As they understood it, they were looking for a baby boy who was lying in a manger somewhere in town.

Unfortunately, they had no idea where this manger-boy might be. After some discussion, they decided they probably shouldn't knock on any more doors.

They were flat stumped for a few minutes, then one of the younger shepherds, a boy named Lemuel, spoke up. "Doesn't old Elias have a manger in his house that he and his wife used as a baby bed?"

"That's right," said Hamran. "My cousin Sarah lives near them. She says they been putting babies in that manger for years."

"That Elias is a strange bird," said another. "Always was. It comes from growing up around Jerusalem. They don't know mangers from menorahs up there."

There were vigorous grunts and nods of approval. Mordecai thumped the table enthusiastically.

Hamran looked thoughtful, then he spoke again. "You know, I heard Sarah talking right before I left for the fields tonight. She was saying something about some young couple having a baby at Elias' house. Esther was helping, along with some other women. These folks was from way out of town. Up Nazareth way, I think. Knowing Elias, I bet that baby's lying in their manger right now."

It was their one and only lead, so they followed it. The whole gang poured outside and ran straight to Esther and Elias' house. When they got there, they found Elias awake, sitting outside his door on a bench. He was understandably startled by their appearance at that hour.

"What are you gang of boys doing here at this time of night. Ain't you supposed to be out watching them sheep?"

There was a pause, then all the shepherds started speaking at once. There was a lot of arm waving and exaggerated gestures. Certainly they were all very excited.

No, he was right there, and . . .

Heard anything like it. He was loud . . .

Singing like you never . . .

Baby's in a trough or maybe eating out of a trough . . .

Swaddling clothes and . . .

Most beautifulest thing you ever heard . . .

Elias listened for a moment, trying to knit it all into something that made sense. Then he shut his eyes tightly and shook his head. "Be quiet, all of you; I can't tell a word you're saying. Not a word of it when you're all talking at once."

He grabbed Lemuel by the shoulders and pulled him forward. "You there, what's your name? Lemuel? Tell me what happened and be clear about it."

"We saw angels when we were with the sheep. They told us about a baby in a manger, that he was a savior and a king. If there's a baby in your house, we come to see him." He paused. "If he's in that manger of yours, that is."

Elias was stunned into silence. He stared at the whole bunch for a few seconds before he spoke. "Well, I never heard anything like that, I must say. Angels? With the sheep? Are you out of your minds? I got a young couple here, just had a baby, got all kinds of family problems and nowhere to stay, and you think I'm going to let you inside just because you say . . ."

"Did they say they saw angels?" interrupted Joseph, who had opened the door and was listening.

Elias whirled around, startled by Joseph's presence. "Well, yes, but I don't think . . ."

"An angel appeared to me in a dream and spoke about this child," announced Joseph calmly.

Elias's mouth hung open a second. Then he clapped it shut.

"And my wife saw an angel too, telling her about our baby. Elias, let them in, if you don't mind. I think they need to see this little boy."

The shepherds filed apologetically past Elias. He mutely watched each of them disappear through the door, which shut behind the last one, leaving him alone outside. He stared at the door for a moment before speaking.

"Well, hell's bells, and I'll dance on Ahab's grave. There ain't a damn thing that's happened here tonight that makes a lick of sense to me."

Part Eight

THE QUESTION

When the shepherds followed Joseph inside, they found Mary lying on a pallet and the baby in a manger made of stones, mortared together with mud and straw. The manger looked well used. Esther had lined the inside with thick layers of cloth.

Like most simple and good-hearted men, the shepherds were keenly aware of holiness and easily awed. Here was a woman's birthing room, a place of mystery and miracle. And here was the child about whom angels sang.

They were uncomfortable and a little afraid. They stood with their feet close together, shoulders curved and heads slightly bowed. Some of them let their hands dangle in front of their groins with one hand grasping the other wrist. There was a lot of shifting from one foot to the other. Two or three knelt.

Elias, who had followed them inside, broke the silence.

"Well, there's the manger you were so keen on seeing. And the little boy." He looked around the room. "Seems like something big is happening, but for the life of me, I can't understand it."

Esther caught his eye and gave him a look that helped him understand he should be quiet. He rolled his eyes and blew air through his lips, but he obeyed.

It was Mary who began talking. She told the story of the heavenly messenger who announced her coming pregnancy. She told them about her family rejecting her and the embarrassment in their hometown.

Joseph told them about the angel from his dream and about the long journey from Nazareth to Bethlehem. He said that Elias had saved them in the alley when they thought all hope was lost.

Esther crinkled her nose at Elias affectionately. He expelled more air from his mouth and tried to look irritated, but he had to turn away so she wouldn't see him smile.

Joseph admitted that neither he nor Mary knew what God had in mind for this little boy. They didn't know, but they had come to believe that he was supposed to be born in this time, and in this place, and even in this way.

"And one more thing," Joseph added. "The angels told us both that we should name him Jesus. The rabbi told me that means, 'God's salvation.'"

Two more of the shepherds knelt. A third started to kneel, then stood back up. He looked around, hesitant, and then knelt after all.

Mordecai nudged one of the other shepherds and nodded his head toward Mary and Joseph. The young man cleared his throat and told them about the angels singing on the hillside. He told them about their fear and the beauty of the angel song and what happened when they tried to tell the good news to the people in town.

Everyone was amazed, even Elias, who kept shaking his head and saying, "I never heard anything like it. Never anything like it in all my life."

Then the little one stirred and all their

The Question

heads turned toward him. Mary lifted him out of the manger. One of the shepherds said, "Can I?" as he reached his hand toward the baby. She nodded, and he held the baby's chin between his thumb and forefinger, grinned, and quickly pulled his hand away.

He was a little boy. A little newborn baby boy and they all felt the common human impulse to "ooh" and "ah." His eyes opened briefly, then shut. His lips moved, searching for something. Mary found a discreet way to move his head beneath a fold in her robe and guide his little mouth to her breast, where he began his first awkward attempts to nurse.

The others turned away politely and began to talk softly among themselves, Joseph last of all.

With this small amount of privacy given her, Mary became absorbed in nursing her child. She prodded the baby's mouth with her nipple as he rooted around, lips opening and closing. Ah, ah, ah, and he was there.

She watched him suckle and gave herself over to the warm sensation and her rising joy. She pondered all she had heard from the angels and the shepherds. She thought about the unlikely events that had brought them to this place.

Her brow crinkled a bit and she tilted her head a little to one side. She looked at her tiny son. His eyes were closed, and he was sucking away in a rhythm.

Then she became the first person to ask the question of the ages. This question would someday split the calendar and define history. This question would bring goodness but also dark evil to humankind. This question would be asked a thousand, thousand times for centuries to come.

"Who are you, my little Jesus boy? Who are you?

The Question